SAYING GOODBYE TO DADDY

JUDITH VIGNA

ALBERT WHITMAN & COMPANY • Morton Grove, Illinois

OTHER BOOKS BY JUDITH VIGNA

Boot Weather

Grandma Without Me

Gregorio y Sus Puntos

I Wish Daddy Didn't Drink So Much

Mommy and Me by Ourselves Again

My Big Sister Takes Drugs

Nobody Wants a Nuclear War

She's Not My Real Mother

Library of Congress Cataloging-in-Publication Data

Vigna, Judith.
Saying goodbye to Daddy / Judith Vigna.
p.   cm.
Summary: Frightened, lonely, and angry after
her father is killed in a car accident, Clare is
helped through the grieving process by her mother
and grandfather.
ISBN 0-8075-7253-5
[1. Death—Fiction.] I. Title.
PZ7.V67Say 1991   90-12757
E—dc20   CIP
#21976344 AC

Text and illustrations © 1991 by Judith Vigna.
Published in 1991 by Albert Whitman & Company,
6340 Oakton Street, Morton Grove, Illinois 60053.
Published simultaneously in Canada
by General Publishing, Limited, Toronto.
All rights reserved. Printed in the U.S.A.
10 9 8 7 6 5 4 3 2 1

The typeface for this book is Goudy Old Style.
The illustration media are watercolor, colored pencil, and ink.

(32)p. 24cm.

TO CHRIS, WITH LOVE,
AND TO OUR FATHERS, REMEMBERED WITH LOVE.

The days that Clare feels very, very sad, her mother makes a pillow of her lap and says, "Let's light the lake house."

She presses a button on the dollhouse Clare's father built the year before he died. A dot of light springs from the tiny lantern by the aluminum foil lake. It flickers and glows. The lake turns gold, and the little carved man in the fishing boat seems to gently rock. Everything is in its place.

The day Clare's father died, nothing was in its place. Instead of her mother, it was Grandfather who fetched her from school. The time was wrong. She hadn't finished lunch. At home, her mother was crying so hard that Clare cried, too. But mostly she was scared.

Mother and Grandfather took her into their circle and Mother said, "A very, very sad thing has happened to Daddy. His car skidded in the rain and fell off the road. He hurt his head so badly that he died."

Clare didn't quite understand. Dying was when petals fell from flowers, leaves fell from trees. When Clare fell and cut her chin, she didn't die.

"Do you remember Sam?" her mother asked. The hamster had grown old and died. When Clare wrapped him to bury him, he was spiny and stiff. Clare had put some cheese into the grave they dug for him. But Mother said he wouldn't eat it. Sam was dead. He wouldn't come alive again. Dead meant not breathing or seeing or feeling cold or hungry or anything at all.

Clare shouted, "It's not true about Daddy!"

Mother and Grandfather nestled her in their arms, and they all cried because the saddest thing had really, truly happened.

At supper, Clare wanted to know, "Where is Daddy now?"

"He's been taken to the funeral home," her mother said quietly. "His body isn't working anymore, so he's going to be buried.

"First he will be dressed in his good blue suit and laid in a casket, a strong, safe box lined with soft fabric. There will be beautiful flowers, and people who loved him will visit to say goodbye. Would you like to come with me to say goodbye?"

"No," Clare said. "Daddy never said goodbye to me." She began to cry. "I didn't mean to drop Daddy's coffee cup. I didn't mean to yell back at him!"

"Oh, no, my darling," Mother said. "Daddy didn't die because you got mad at him. The car accident caused it. He wasn't always patient, but he loved you for helping to wash the dishes."

A lot of relatives came to the house that night. There was hugging and kissing, and the room was full of sadness and love.

Clare felt sad and scared inside, but she wanted to help serve cookies.

One chocolate chip cookie she saved for her father. Those had been his favorite. She would ask her mother to put it in the casket even if he couldn't eat it.

While her mother was at the funeral home the next day, Grandfather stayed with Clare. "Do you feel like playing with the lake house?" he asked.

"I *hate* the lake house. I wish it would burn all up!" Clare pulled the tiny man from his fishing boat and smashed him, head down, into the foil waves. Then she snatched the lantern from its post to stop the twinkling.

Grandfather's broad hand closed over hers, but she tugged away. He wasn't angry. "I brought your favorite soda," he said. "Why don't we drink some on the porch?"

Clare and Grandfather waited on the porch for Mother to come home.

"Frank looked so peaceful in the casket," Mother told Grandfather. She bent to kiss Clare, but Clare shook her head. "I don't like you all the time!" she yelled.

Mother cried softly because she was tired and sad. Grandfather explained, "Mommy can't be with you as much as she'd like. She has to spend time at the funeral home with the people who've come to say goodbye to Daddy."

"What if you and Mommy die, too?"

Her mother hugged her. "I expect to live a long, long time, longer than you can imagine. Pop's health is fine. And if anything happened to us, Aunt Helen and Uncle Jim would take care of you."

"Will I live a long time?"

"I expect so," Mother said. Clare hugged her back.

The next night, Grandfather said, "Daddy's getting buried in the morning. Do you want to go to the church and the cemetery with Mommy and me? If you don't, Aunt Helen will stay with you."

"I think I do," Clare said. She wasn't quite sure what a cemetery looked like, except for stones like rows of teeth with people's names on them.

Grandfather put on a proper black suit, and a veil covered Mother's hair. Clare chose her favorite red dress.

Riding to the church made her afraid. She hadn't forgotten how her father died. Mother kissed her. "I'm a bit scared, too," she said. "But most cars don't crash, and our driver's very careful."

Her father's casket was at the church altar, sheltered by armfuls of flowers. The minister talked for a long time, and so she wouldn't get bored, Clare counted all the times he said her father's name, Franklin Johns. Everyone sang and cried.

They even laughed once, when the minister told how her father had built a bird apartment house so each bird in the garden had its own place to feed.

When the minister finished, some men held the casket by its thick brass handles and wheeled it to a black, shiny car called a hearse. The limousine that held Clare and Mother and Grandfather joined the ribbon of cars to the cemetery.

Clare whispered, "What if Daddy gets cold and hungry? How will he get out of the casket?"

Grandfather's hand covered her head like a cap. "Daddy's dead, sweetheart. He can't feel anything. His body doesn't work anymore."

"But where do people go when they die?"

"I don't know for sure," Grandfather said. "The minister says Daddy's in heaven. But whatever people believe, the memory of how someone lived stays on after that person has died. The good, kind, clever things your Daddy did will live through you and be remembered by everyone who loved him."

Clare watched the men rest her father's casket over the deep hole where it would be buried. The minister spoke, and some mourners sniffled. Grandfather's eyes were closed, and his lips made sounds no one could hear.

Crying, Mother kissed one of two red roses she was holding and placed it on the casket. The other rose she gave to Clare. Clare peeled off its thorn and set the flower down beside her mother's.

Then the minister sprinkled some earth on the casket. It fell on the satiny wood with a pattering sound, reminding Clare of chocolate chips. She was glad she'd asked her mother to put a cookie inside the casket because chocolate chip cookies were her father's favorite when he lived and was able to eat.

Still, it was hard to say goodbye.

Grandfather stayed with Clare and Mother for a long time after the funeral, but Clare sometimes felt lonely. Downstairs, Grandfather napped and did crossword puzzles. Upstairs, Mother napped and wept. Some afternoons Clare took off her shoes and crept into bed with her.

"The hurt will go away," Grandfather promised. "We won't always feel sad all the time."

One afternoon, Clare's mother came downstairs and said, "I found some things in Daddy's wallet. He saved everything. He was such a little boy sometimes!"

Clare giggled. "That's silly, Mommy. Daddy was old. Not old like Pop, but much, much older than me."

They sat together on the rug and pecked through the things spread there.

A ticket stub.

"Remember the baseball game Daddy took you to last summer? Would you believe he saved this? He loved taking you places."

A clipping from the newspaper about the kindergarten play. *Clare Johns was a magnificent rabbit.*

"Daddy was so proud of you."

There was a calendar Clare had made. It wasn't even the right year, but her father had kept it all the same.

"Daddy always said you inherited your talent for making things from him."

"That's me!" Clare waved an old photograph of herself with her father. "Don't I look like him, Mommy?"

Her mother smiled. "Daddy carried your picture with him always. Right in the pocket next to his heart." She patted the left side of Clare's chest. "He loved you so much."

Grandfather snorted into his handkerchief. "Anyone want to help me fix the lake house?"

"I'll race you upstairs," Clare said.

The nights that Clare feels very, very sad, her mother says, "Let's light the lake house." She presses a button, and a dot of light springs from the tiny lantern by the aluminum foil lake. The light spills over Clare's pillow with the leathery bump of her father's wallet beneath.

Mother kisses her. "Goodnight, my darling girl."

"Goodnight, Mommy."

Clare sees the dark beyond the door as her mother leaves the room, but she feels safe.

"Goodbye, Daddy," she says.